THE LOST LEGACY

MISSING OF A VALUABLE HEIRLOOM

VISHVA.K

Contents

Prologue

ARE YOU READY FOR A RIDE OF A LIFE TIME LETS GO ON ANTOINE AND DUSTINS JORNEY TO FIND ANTOINESLOST LEGACY HIS MISSING HEIRLOOM !

AND

ABISHEK TO FIND HIS PARENTS

AND

JOHN TO SAVE HIS CITY FROM THE ORDER!

THE LOST LEGACY 1

Antoines heirloom:

In the city of Paris, a wealthy art collector named Antoine was in possession of a rare and valuable heirloom, a diamond encrusted brooch passed down through generations of the family. But one day, the brooch went missing and Antoine found himself at the center of a mysterious and dangerous game.

Desperate to recover the brooch and uncover the truth behind its disappearance, Antoine turned to a young private investigator named Dustin. Despite his young age and lack of experience, Dustin had a reputation for being smart, resourceful, and fearless, and Antoine believed he was the only one who could help him.

Together, they set out to solve the mystery and retrieve the missing heirloom. Their journey took them from the elegant mansions of Paris to the dark alleys of the city's criminal underworld, as they followed a track of clues that led them deeper into the dangerous and mysterious world of art theft.

As they delved deeper into the investigation, they discovered that the brooch was much more than just a valuable piece of jewelry. It held the key to a dark and dangerous secret, and now, a dangerous criminal organization known as The Shadow Syndicate was after it.

Dustin and Antoine found themselves caught in a deadly game of cat and mouse, as they raced against time to find the brooch and uncover the truth before The Shadow Syndicate could get to it. They faced impossible odds and dangerous obstacles, but their determination and bravery led them to a shocking discovery.

The brooch was part of a larger puzzle, leading them to an ancient and powerful artifact known as the Mind Control Device. And now, The Shadow Syndicate was determined to use the artifact for their own purposes, to gain control over the minds of powerful leaders and politicians, and to rule the world from the shadows.

As they delved deeper into the mystery, Dustin and Antoine found themselves in a race against time to prevent The Shadow Syndicate from acquiring the device and using it for their evil purposes. They encountered dangerous and powerful enemies, including the enigmatic and dangerous leader of The Shadow Syndicate, known only as The Shadow king.

In a final showdown, Dustin and Antoine found themselves face-to-face with The Shadow king and his followers, and they were forced to make a choice. To keep the artifact and the power it held, or to destroy it and risk everything.

In the end, their bravery and determination led them to a shocking conclusion, and they discovered that the true value of the heirloom was not in its material worth, but in the strength and courage it took to protect it.Dustin and Antoine emerged from the dangerous adventure as heroes, their names forever remembered as the ones who stood up against the forces of evil and saved the world from the shadow of tyranny.

CHAPTER TWO

THE LOST LEGACY 2

Abisheks lost heirloom his parents:

Abishek had always felt like something was missing from his life. Growing up, he was adopted by loving parents and had a happy childhood, but he couldn't shake off the feeling that he needed to know his roots. He had a burning desire to know who his biological parents were and where he came from.

One day, while going through some old family albums, he stumbled upon a picture of a couple who looked familiar to him. It was like a sign that he needed to search for answers. He hired a private investigator and after months of searching, he finally uncovered the truth about his past.

Abishek's parents were part of a wealthy and powerful family, but his mother was disowned after she fell in love with a man from a lower social class. Sadly, his parents were murdered shortly after Abishek was born, and the crime was never solved.

Determined to bring justice to his parents and uncover the truth about their deaths, Abishek dug deep into the family's dark secrets. He soon realized that his quest for answers was putting him in grave danger. He began receiving threatening letters and his home was broken into multiple times.

Fearing for his life, Abishek had reached out to a former detective who had been investigating his parents' case for years. Together, they uncovered a web of deceit and corruption that went all the way to the top of the family's hierarchy.

The final showdown had taken place in the family's mansion, where Abishek and the detective confronted the mastermind behind his parents' murder. In a pulse-pounding confrontation, they finally brought the killer to justice.

Abishek's journey had come full circle, and he finally found peace knowing that his parents' deaths were avenged. But as he walked away from the mansion, he couldn't shake off the feeling that someone was still watching him, waiting for the right moment to strike again.

Abishek's quest for the truth had led him down a dark and dangerous path. But he was driven by a sense of justice for his parents and a desire to know the truth about his past.

After the showdown at the family mansion, Abishek was shaken to the core. He had uncovered secrets that would have been better left buried, and he couldn't shake off the feeling that he was still in danger. He confided in the former detective, who advised him to go into hiding until the dust had settled.

Abishek followed the detective's advice and disappeared without a trace. He lived a quiet life in a small town, using a fake identity to keep a low profile. But even in hiding, he couldn't escape his past. Mysterious letters continued to arrive, and he felt like he was being watched at all times.

One night, while walking home from the local store, he was accosted by two masked men. They grabbed him, threw him into a van, and drove him to an abandoned warehouse on the outskirts of town. There, he was confronted by the leader of the family, who revealed that the threats against Abishek were far from over.

The leader told Abishek that the family would stop at nothing to protect their secrets and that he was a loose end that needed to be tied up. In that moment, Abishek realized that he was in grave danger and that he had to find a way to escape.

Using his quick thinking and determination, Abishek managed to overpower his captors and escape into the night. He went on the run, determined to bring down the corrupt family once and for all. He worked with the former detective to gather evidence and build a case against the family, using his insider knowledge to stay one step ahead of them.

After months of living in hiding and gathering evidence, Abishek finally had enough to bring down the family. In a dramatic courtroom showdown, he took the stand and exposed the family's corruption, bringing them to justice once and for all.

In the end, Abishek finally found peace knowing that his parents' deaths were avenged and that the truth about his past had been uncovered. He could finally move on with his life, free from the shadows of the past.

CHAPTER THREE

THE LOST LEGACY 3

john saving his heirloom his city:

In a small town, a string of mysterious disappearances had been plaguing the community for months. The local police were stumped, with no leads or suspects in sight. But one person wasn't giving up so easily.

Meet John, a young and determined reporter who was determined to uncover the truth behind these disappearances. He dug deep, interviewing witnesses and scouring the town for any evidence that might help crack the case.

One day, John received an anonymous tip about a strange, cloaked figure seen lurking around the area where several of the disappearances had taken place. Despite the danger

John was not one to back down from a challenge, and this case was no exception. With his sharp mind and relentless determination, he was determined to get to the bottom of this mystery, no matter what it took.

He started by talking to anyone and everyone who had information about the disappearances. He interviewed witnesses, visited the families of the missing, and scoured the town for any clues that might lead him in the right direction. As he gathered more and more information, John began to piece together a disturbing pattern that seemed to be emerging.

One day, John had received an anonymous tip about a strange, cloaked figure that had been seen lurking around the area where several of the disappearances had taken place. Despite the danger, John was determined to follow this lead and see where it would take him.

As he dug deeper, John began to uncover a web of deceit and corruption that ran throughout the town. He discovered that the key to solving the disappearances lay with a secret society, known only as "The Order," who held great power and influence over the town and its residents. The members of this society were rumored to be involved in all sorts of illegal activities, including the disappearances.

John knew he was getting close to the truth, but he also knew that he was putting himself in great danger. The members of "The Order" were not the kind of people you wanted to cross, and they would stop at nothing to keep their secrets safe. But John was not deterred. He was determined to bring the truth to light and put an end to this mystery once and for all.

As he continued his investigation, John found himself being followed, and he knew that he was running out of time. He had to act fast before it was too late. With a plan in mind, John made his move and confronted the members of "The Order." In a tense standoff, John managed to extract a confession from the leader of the society, revealing all of the secrets behind the disappearances.

Thanks to John's bravery and determination, the truth was finally brought to light, and the families of the missing finally received the answers they had been searching for. John's name became synonymous with courage and integrity, and he was hailed as a hero by the entire town and the people in it.

தனிமையின் தூாரிகை

நந்தினி தேவி

என் திறமையை வெளிக்கொணர வேண்டி என்னை ஊக்குவித்த என்
பெற்றோர்களுக்கும்

என் நண்பர்களுக்கும் சமர்ப்பணம்.

பொருளடக்கம்

அணிந்துரை

இந்த புத்தகத்தில் இடம்பெற்றுள்ள ஒவ்வொரு கவிதையும் வாழ்கையை சார்ந்த

வேறு வேறு தலைப்பில் இடம் பெற்றிருக்கும்.

மேலும் எளிதில் புரிந்து கொள்ளும் வகையிலேயே இடம்பெற்றிருக்கும்.

முன்னுரை

வணக்கம் வாசகர்களே!!!

இந்த நூல் ஒரு கவிதை தொகுப்பு. இன்றைய கால கட்டத்தில் கவிதை வாசிப்பவர்கள்

மிகவும் குறைவு என்றாலும் கவிதை மீது நான் கொண்ட தீரா காதலால்

இந்நூலை வெளியிடுகிறேன்.....

இது என் முதல் நூல் என்பதால் என் கவிதைகளில் 5 கவிதைகளை மட்டுமே

இந்த தொகுப்பில் வெளியிடுகிறேன்.....வாசகர்கள் இதில் பிழை ஏதும் இருந்தால் மன்னித்துக்கொள்ளவும்.

என்னுடைய சொந்த குரலில் நான் @thanimayin_thoorigai_ என்ற இன்ஸ்டாகிராம் பக்-கத்தில்

கவிதைகளை கூறியுள்ளேன் நீங்கள் விருப்பப்பட்டால் இந்த ஐடியை பின்பற்றி கவிதைகளை

என் குரலில் கேட்கலாம்.

நன்றி

இந்த நூலை நான் உருவாக்க என்னை ஊக்குவித்த என் பெற்றோருக்கும்,

என் நண்பர்களுக்கும்.....

எனது மனமார்ந்த நன்றி!

அத்தியாயம்1

புத்தகம்.....

அறியாத வயதில் நான் அழகிய எழுத்துக்களை அறிந்ததும் உன்-
னால் தான்.

அமுது போன்ற மொழி தமிழ் என நான் உணர்ந்ததும் உன்னால்
தான்.

நான் எழுதுகின்ற கவிதைகள் ஒவ்வொன்றும் நீ கற்று தந்த
பாடங்களே.

பட்டப்படிப்புகள் படித்த பின்னும்.....

புதிதாய் வாங்கிய உன் மணம்.....

அதை என் மனம் விரும்புதே.....

நான் திருப்பிய உன் ஒவ்வொரு பக்கமும்.....

என் வாழ்வில் புதிய திருப்பத்தை தந்ததே.....

நான் விலை கொடுத்து வாங்கிய.....

என் புத்தகமே.....!

அத்தியாயம்2

அவளும் விடியலும்.....

அழகிய பதுமை அவள்!!!

ஆயிரம் முறை தோற்றுப்போய் ஆயிரத்தொன்றாவது முறை எழுந்து நின்றாள்.....

அழாதே என்று கூறி அவள் கண்ணீர் துடைக்க அருகில் யாரும் இல்லை,

அச்சம் என்பது சிறிதும் இன்றி,

வழியும் கண்ணீரை தன் பூ போன்ற மெல்லிய கரங்களால் துடைத்தாள்.....

சிந்திய கண்ணீர் துளிகள் அனைத்தும் வைரமாய் மின்ன,

தன் மனம் கூறிய திசை நோக்கி நடை போட்டாள்.....

புதியதொரு விடியலை தேடி!

அத்தியாயம் 3

பயணம்.....

மனிதன் தேடும் மாற்றங்கள் அனைத்தும்

மண் மீது தவழும் இயற்கையின் வடிவமே!

உன் விழி திறந்து நீ காணும் ஒவ்வொரு விடியலும்,

உன் உயிரினை புதுப்பிக்கும் அற்புதமே!!

சோகம் எனும் சுமை அதை சற்று விலக்கிடவே.....

காற்றோடு காற்றாக கலந்து நகர்ந்திடு.....

கரை உடைத்து செல்லும் வெள்ளம் போல,

உன் மனம் திறந்து நீயும் பயணித்திடு!!!

அத்தியாயம்4

கவிதைக்கு ஒரு கவிதை.....
நான் காண இயலா நிஜங்களின் கனவு நீ!
அந்த கனவெனும் ஆழ்கடலின்.....
பிரதிபிம்பம் நீ!
நான் காற்றோடு கதை பேச காரணம் நீ!
என் வாழ்க்கை எனும் காகிதத்தில் பூக்கும்.....
கவிதை எனும் மலர்வனம் நீயே!

அத்தியாயம்5

மாற்றம்.....
மாற்றங்கள் யாவையும் மாற்றுவதென்பது,
முடியாத ஒன்று.....!
மாறிய யாவையும் ஏற்றுக்கொண்டு,
மனம் விரும்பிய திசை நோக்கி,
பயணிக்க தொடங்கு,
உன் புதிய பாதையில்.....!